The Tiger Who Was A ROARING SUCCESS!

DON CONROY

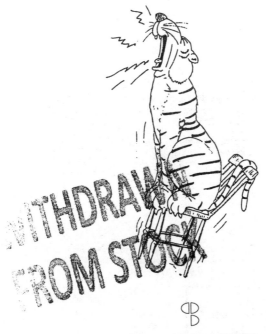

THE O'BRIEN PRESS
DUBLIN

This revised and redesigned edition first published 1994
by The O'Brien Press Ltd.,
20 Victoria Road, Rathgar, Dublin 6, Ireland.
Tel: +353 1 4923333; Fax: +353 1 4922777
E-mail: books@obrien.ie
Website: www.obrien.ie
Reprinted 1998.

ISBN 0-86278-371-2

British Library Cataloguing-in-Publication Data
Conroy, Don. Tiger Who Was a Roaring Success. - new Ed.
I. Title
823.914 [J]

5   6   7   8   9   10
01   02   03   04   05   06

Typesetting, layout, editing, design: The O'Brien Press Ltd.
Cover illustrations: Don Conroy
Cover separations: Lithoset Ltd.
Printing: Guernsey Press Ltd.

Barny owl was flying home. It had been a long night's hunting, and he was looking forward to a good sleep.

'I'd better hurry up,' he said to himself, 'or Billy will start up.'

The sun would soon be up and Billy Blackbird would begin the dawn chorus. Billy took this job *very seriously* and was never late.

He would start it, then the robins, wrens, chaffinches, thrushes and even the swallows would join in. In seconds they would all be twittering away in the hedges and on the wires.

That would put an end to any sleep for Barny!

Barny liked to be asleep before the day birds got going. But tonight he was late home.

I went just that bit too far, he thought. He was exhausted.

Finally, he saw the walls of the old castle ruin where he lived, and he flapped his wings quickly.

Not a peep from Billy yet! I might just make it, Barny thought.

He glided straight over the wall and in through a small window. He ruffled his feathers and closed his eyes.

'Home at last!' He stretched and yawned.

Then it started! Billy was on time as usual. Soon the whole place was filled with sound.

'Oh no! Now it'll be ages before I get to sleep,' moaned Barny.

Suddenly there was a roar. A very *strange* roar. The loudest roar Barny had ever heard.

What was *that*? Who could make such a noise? he wondered. There would definitely be no sleep now.

He wanted to hide, but his curiosity got the better of him and he just *had* to find out what or who had made that terrible noise.

He listened. There wasn't a sound to be heard. No more dawn chorus! Even Billy had stopped.

Then Barny heard something shuffling. Something was coming up the wall of his home!

He couldn't see a thing, but his keen hearing could detect the smallest sound. He began to shake all over. It must be some kind of monster!

It was getting closer and closer!

He decided to make a run for it and flew to the window – only to crash into his best friend Sammy Squirrel.

'Oooouch!' they both shouted.

'Oh! It's only you!' said Barny.

'What do you mean *only* me?' said Sammy, picking himself up.

'Was that you?' asked Barny.

'Of course it's me.'

'For a moment,' said Barny, 'I thought it was a monster.'

'Me? A monster! Thanks very much.'

'Do it again,' said Barny.

Sammy looked at Barny. He *was* behaving oddly. 'Well, if you insist,' said Sammy, and he fell back on the floor.

'No, not *that*, silly, that roar.'

'It was more like an ooouch!' said Sammy.

'You didn't make a roar?'

'No.'

'Then it's a monster.'

'That's why I came here,' said Sammy, 'to tell you about the roar.'

'But I *knew* about the roar,' said Barny, 'didn't I just ask you about it?'

'Let's start again,' said Sammy, completely confused by now.

Suddenly they heard another loud, piercing roar.

'There it goes again,' said Sammy.

'What'll we do?' asked Barny.

'We'll all have a meeting at Three Rock at twilight to talk about it,' said Sammy, who always got everyone organised. That evening all the animals met. Renny Fox opened the meeting.

'It seems we have a strange creature in our woods. Has anyone seen it?'

'No,' came the answer.

'But,' said Bentley Badger . . .

'*You* have?' they all said, trembling with fear.

'Is it a monster?' asked Barny.

'I didn't see it,' said Bentley. 'But I saw a *huge* footprint near my sett.'

Now, everyone knew that Bentley's own footprints were the biggest in the woods.

'Bigger than yours?' said Harry. 'Then Barny's right. It must be a monster.'

Suddenly there was a loud roar. Everyone dived for cover. Barny

shrieked and hid in a tree.

A long shadow appeared on the ground and two yellow eyes shone in the gathering darkness.

Harry, who had rolled into a ball, opened one eye – and there was the biggest cat he had ever seen!

'It's a giant cat!' he yelled.

The cat moved towards him. Harry closed his eyes, expecting

the worst. The creature sniffed at him, but Harry held his shape, hoping his prickles would protect him. Then he heard a big, loud voice.

'Please don't be afraid. I only want to be friends.'

Harry wasn't sure he could trust the stranger. Slowly he unfolded his body, gazing all the time at the giant cat.

'Y-y-you're n-n-not going to eat me?' he stuttered.

The cat looked sad.

'No,' he said. 'I only want to talk to somebody.'

Harry decided to trust this stranger – he looked kind.

'Okay, everybody,' he shouted, 'it's okay to come out.'

They all came out slowly, Billy Blackbird last of all because he was still a bit suspicious.

'Sorry for frightening you all,' said the stranger. 'You see, I'd forgotten how loud my roar is! My name is Bengal. I'm an escapee.'

'You look like a cat to me,' said Harry.

'Oh, I *am* a cat,' agreed Bengal.

'But I thought you just said you were a scrapee or something!' said Harry.

'I've escaped from the circus,' said Bengal. 'I'm an escapee. I want to go home to India.'

'A circus? What's that? And where's India?' asked Sammy.

'Well, let me explain everything. You see, I'm a tiger – that's a large cat – from a place called India, which is very far away from here.'

'And did you walk all the way?' asked Harry admiringly.

'Oh no! When I was a cub . . .'

'A *cub*! Were you in the scouts?' Harry had often seen the cubs in the woods on Sundays.

'No! I mean when I was *little* – a cub – a terrible thing happened,' said Bengal. They were all listening now. 'One day I was out in the lovely warm jungle with my mother. And I fell into a big hole that was covered with long leaves, so I did't see it.

'I sat in the dark, deep hole for ages. My mother tried everything to get me out. She was even going to jump into the hole herself, but it would have been impossible to jump out again.'

'No point in two of you getting stuck,' agreed Harry.

'If I was there,' said Sammy

fiercely, 'I would have pushed those men into the hole!'

'You wouldn't have been able,' said Billy wisely.

'Let him tell his story,' said Bentley.

'Then we heard a heavy footfall,' went on Bengal. 'Then four men came, waving fire sticks and they chased my mother away. Then a net was thrown over me and I was hauled out and carried off.'

He wiped his nose and sighed. 'I was put in a small, dark box . . .'

'Wow!' said Harry. 'First a hole, then a net, then a box . . . '

'Harry, would you *please* let him finish,' said Billy.

'Then the box was loaded onto a ship with lots of other boxes with animals in them. And  there I was heading for . . . well I didn't know where.'

The animals all had tears in their eyes. They had never heard such a sad story.

'Then a circus owner bought me,'

continued Bengal. 'And I became part of a circus act. I had to jump over stools and roll over.

'I had to sit on tiny chairs. And it wasn't just me – there were lions

there from Africa, and cheetahs, and leopards. The trainer had a whip and he would lay it hard across our backs if we disobeyed. And we had to live in small cages.'

'That's terrible,' said Renny. Everyone nodded.

'After a while I became very good at rolling over and jumping through hoops of fire. And my special act was to make a loud roar. In fact, I became a roaring success! I was the most popular animal in the circus.

'But I got tired of it all. So I decided to try to escape. I waited and waited for my chance. I waited ten years for it.

'Then last week when we were driving in our truck from one town to another we had a crash. My cage turned over and the door opened.

'I got out as fast as I could, leaped over a hedge and ran into the woods. That's how I came here,' said Bengal.

'That was very brave,' said Barny.

'Yes, I suppose it was,' agreed Bengal proudly. 'I come from a very noble and brave race of tigers.'

'They'll be looking for you,' said Billy.

'Do you think so?' asked Bengal, beginning to tremble.

'Definitely!' said Billy. 'Especially if you were so popular.'

'Oh, why did I have to be popular? Of course, I can't help it if I *am* good at things,' Bengal said proudly. 'You know, all my family were successful. Take my uncle, now . . . ' He was just about to tell them when he saw a big black shadow behind him. 'Help! Save me!' he screamed.

'What is it?' asked Ollie.

'A huge big shadow sneaked up behind me,' said Bengal. 'Look.

Over there. Oh, it's gone. Well, it was definitely there! As big as me.'

'It *was* you,' said Billy.

'Oops!' said Bengal. 'Imagine being afraid of my own shadow!'

The animals laughed. It *was* strange that such a big animal could be scared so easily! Well, he had had a hard life . . .

'I don't want to go back to the circus,' said Bengal. 'Well, you can stay here as long as you like,' said Harry, and they all agreed.

'That's very nice of you all,' said Bengal. 'I'd love to stay a while, but I must get home to my family in India. Sometimes I get news from a swallow who became my friend after I let him use my cage to build his nest in. Every summer he brings me news. He always visits me, wherever I am.'

'Well, we would help you get to India, if we only knew where it was,' said Bentley Badger.

'That's the problem,' said Bengal.

'*I* don't know where it is either.'

'Then, that's a *real* problem,' said Billy seriously, from his perch in a tree above the tiger. 'I'll have to think about this.'

They all thought about it.

Then Sammy had an idea. 'Why don't we go to Old Lepus?'

'Who's that?' asked Bengal.

'An old hare who once lived with people,' explained Renny. 'He knows more than anyone, even Billy.'

Billy wasn't sure how to take that.

'Shush!' said Barny, suddenly. 'I hear something! Hide!'

Lights flashed in the dark. Men!

'He must be around here somewhere,' shouted one of them.

'He'll get this whip across his back when I find him,' said another.

They went off in different directions – luckily the *wrong* directions.

Nobody moved for a while, then everyone came out slowly.

'Nasty lot,' said Harry. 'They're the ones who should be in cages.'

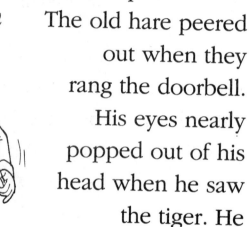

They all set off to find Old Lepus.

The old hare peered out when they rang the doorbell. His eyes nearly popped out of his head when he saw the tiger. He slammed the door shut.

Sammy rang the bell again. 'It's only a tiger, Lepus.'

'What do you mean – *only* a tiger! Tigers belong in jungles, not here

in the woods. Kindly take him
back where he belongs.'

'I will not go back,' said Bengal.

'Please let us explain,' said
Renny. And he told Old Lepus the
whole story.

'Imagine that!' said Lepus. 'Well, I
suppose it's nice to have foreign
visitors. Now let me see . . .' and
he went off inside and got an atlas.

He spread it out on the grass and pointed to India.

'It's very far away,' said Old Lepus. 'Days and days on a ship.' He showed them the seas Bengal would have to cross. 'Now, how could we possibly get you there?' he wondered.

He drew a map and showed them all how to get to the harbour

where the ships would be ready to sail.

'But there's one big problem,' he said, looking at Bengal. 'Your stripes.'

Bengal looked at his stripes. He was rather proud of them.

'They're a real giveaway,' said Lepus. 'You'd be spotted a mile away. We'll have to disguise you.'

'I know!' piped up Harry. 'We could cover him with leaves and pretend he's a big bush!'

'That's silly,' said Sammy. 'The

wind would blow them all away.'

'Cover him with mud?' suggested
Bentley.

'No. It cracks when
it dries,' said Renny.

We all thought hard.

'I know!' said Sammy. 'Flour!'

'Now, that's *really* silly,' said
Harry. 'Where would you get a
flower big enough?'

'Not a flower, dummy, *flour*,' said
Sammy. 'White flour. We'll make
him look like a big white pet dog.'

'Not bad,' agreed Billy.
'But where do we get it?'

'Over at the bakery near Malone's farm,' said Sammy. 'I saw a dog there once, covered in flour. He looked like a snow dog!'

'But how do we get the flour back here?' asked Billy. 'We'll need a lot to cover him.'

'Why doesn't he just go with you?' suggested Old Lepus.

'Of course,' they all agreed.

'But you must all have some supper first,' said Old Lepus. 'How about apple and blackberry pie?'

They sat outside in the warm starry night, eating pie and lapping spring water.

Bengal managed twelve pies, six honey cakes and a barrel of cool spring water. And Old Lepus didn't mind his food store being cleared out by this unusual guest. Harry climbed *into* his pie and ate it from the centre out! He looked quite silly with blackberry and apple all over his face. He tried to clean himself with his paws, but got more and more messy. When Bengal offered to help, Harry looked surprised. But one lick of the tiger's tongue cleaned Harry's face, and he looked very pleased.

By now everyone was sleepy. There would be no flour hunt tonight! Billy was already snoring under some ferns. Sammy was dozing, and then Bengal gave a loud yawn which startled them all.

'Oops!' he said. 'I'm feeling rather sleepy after that lovely supper.'

They thanked old Lepus and headed home. Barny was the only one feeling wide awake and he went off for a quiet flight over the fields.

They took
Bengal to the
Three Rock
where he could
sleep under a
boulder that lay
across a ditch.
There were plenty of
nettles and brambles across the
entrance to cover him. Bengal
stretched, yawned again and
settled into a deep sleep.

What nobody
knew was that the
men had laid traps
to catch the tiger!
But they soon
found out when

Harry fell into
a deep pit
covered with
branches and
leaves, just
like the one
Bengal had
spoken of in
India. Then Barny flew into a net
that was stretched across the trees!
And Ollie fell into a pit – but *he*
managed to climb out.

Bentley and Renny saw none of
this happening. But they did get a
strong scent of humans near the
sett where the badger lived. They
both circled round, sniffing the air.
Then there was a loud snap! and

Bentley screeched in pain. Renny froze with fear. Then he rushed to Bentley. Poor Bentley was in real trouble, his leg caught in a steel trap. Renny tried to release it but it was too tight.

'Who would do this?' cried Bentley. 'And why?'

'It must be the men looking for Bengal,' said Renny. 'You stay here and I'll go for help . . . Oh, sorry, I suppose you can't go anywhere!'

'I certainly can't!' said Bentley, trying to be brave.

Renny rushed off, only to meet Ollie Otter trying to free poor Barny from the net. The net was too strong to bite through.

'Hold on, Barny, we'll get help,' said Renny. 'Come on, Ollie.'

The two of them ran off through the woods – and soon discovered Harry *and* Sammy Squirrel in a deep pit!

'Oh no, not you two as well!' moaned Renny.

'Oh, *I'm* okay,' said Sammy, and he scrambled up the earth. 'It's poor Harry. I just can't get him out.'

'This is terrible,' said Bentley. 'But maybe we have the answer. Let's get Bengal!'

The big tiger was still sleeping soundly, dreaming of India.

He heard a noise. Oh no! I'll be caught again! he thought, and he began to shake all over.

'Hello, Bengal, wake up,' said a friendly voice. It was Renny.

Bengal was delighted to find it was his friends.

'Anything wrong?' he asked.

'Plenty,' said Ollie. 'The men laid traps for you.'

'I thought they might,' said Bengal, 'but don't worry – I'm safe.'

'Yes, but Barny, Harry and Bentley are caught!'

'What!' said Bengal, leaping up. 'Where are they? Come on, we must rescue them.'

They ran to Harry. He was looking very cheerful, now he was sure that they'd free him.

'How will we manage this?' wondered Bengal.

'Maybe you could climb down and get him out?' suggested Renny.

But Bengal was afraid he might not be able to get back up.

'I'm not sure,' he said. 'Let's see . . . I'll have to use my head here.'

'Why don't you use your tail instead?' shouted Harry.

That was it! Of course! Bengal turned around and backed carefully towards the pit.

44

Then he let down his long tail. Harry jumped from the gound – and *missed*!

'Can you hold your tail still?' said Harry. 'It's moving all over the place. I can't get a grip.'

'I'll try,' said Bengal. 'But it seems to have a mind of its own.'

He closed his eyes and began to think of his tail. Slowly it grew still, apart from the very tip which curled up and twitched.

But Harry still couldn't jump high enough.

Bengal edged back closer to the hole. His strong paws had a firm grip on the grass.

Closer and closer he went.

'Got it!' yelled Harry at last.

But the tail, with Harry on it, started to swing!

Bengal gripped madly at the grass, clawing his way from the hole.

'Come on!' shouted Renny, grabbing Bengal's paw. 'Pull!'

At last Bengal made it. He dragged himself and Harry out of the hole.

'Hurrah!' they all shouted.

Bengal was pleased. 'Now let's go to Barny!' he said.

There was Barny, covered in netting. 'Hello, everyone, I'm still tied up here!' he shouted. 'But my friend Otus came to keep me company.'

The long-eared brown owl sat chatting to Barny.

'You know, all these traps were laid for you,' said Otus to Bengal.

'Indeed I do,' said Bengal. 'And you've all got caught! Terrible!'

He opened his huge jaws and snapped fiercely at the netting. Barny couldn't help being frightened at the tiger's jaws, even though he knew Bengal was his friend. He hid his head under his wing and waited, shaking.

Bengal chewed and chewed at the cord.

'It doesn't taste very nice,' he mumbled. At last he managed to

chew a large hole in
the net. 'That should
do it. Come
on, Barny.'

Barny lifted
his head and
walked out of the
net. 'Oh, thanks, Bengal,' he said.
He shook himself and flapped his
wings.

'Think nothing of it,' said Bengal.
'It's because of me you were there
in the first place. Anyway, my
mother always said "If you can't do
a good deed, don't do a bad one".'

'There's still another good deed
to be done!' said Renny.

Off they ran to find Bentley.

He was lying quietly on the
ground, scared.

'Is anything broken?'
asked Bengal.

'I'm not sure,' said
Bentley, 'but it's
very painful.'
'This is all my fault!'
said Bengal again.

Carefully he gripped the cold
steel in his teeth and with his left
paw he pulled the trap open.

Everyone cheered.

Bentley licked his leg.

'Can you walk?' asked Ollie.

The badger tried but it was too
painful.

'Let's take him to Old Lepus. He'll

fix it,' said Sammy.

'I don't think I could get that far,' said Bentley.

'Allow me the honour of carrying you,' said Bengal, and he lay down as flat as he could on the ground.

By now all the animals were beginning to like Bengal. He wasn't so boastful or proud anymore.

Bentley climbed up on his back. Then Sammy leaped onto the tiger's head. 'I hope you don't mind,' he shouted.

'Not at all!' said Bengal. 'Now that you're up there, would you mind scratching behind my left ear – no, the *other* one – that's it. Oh, that's great.'

'Is there room for me?' asked Harry.

Bengal nodded and Harry scrambled up.

'We're off!' shouted Bengal.

He set off at a fast pace through the woods. Renny and Ollie raced along after him and Barny flew above their heads with Otus.

Old Lepus was surprised to see them all back so soon. He brought Bentley in and put him on the table.

'Hmmmm! Looks quite sore,' he mumbled. 'Not broken, luckily.'

He bathed the leg in warm water with some special herbs from his store, and Bentley began to feel better already. Then Old Lepus took down a jar of comfrey cream and rubbed it onto the badger's leg.

'You were lucky,' he said to Bentley. 'All you need now is rest.'

'I think that goes for us all!' said Harry. 'Can we stay here, Lepus?'

'Make yourselves at home,' said the old hare, and they all settled in to rest until morning.

*   *   *

At sun-up, Billy Blackbird started the dawn chorus.

'Time to go,' he called.

They all set off for the bakery to find the flour to disguise Bengal. Bengal was a bit nervous.

'I hope we don't bump into any of those men,' he said.

They crept through the fields, watching carefully. Then Bengal stopped dead. 'Look!' He pointed. 'Dogs everywhere. And they've covered themselves with white flour! But they don't fool *me*!'

'But they're not dogs,' said Harry, 'they're *sheep*. Harmless animals.'

'Oh,' said Bengal, feeling a bit silly.

'Anyone could make that mistake if they hadn't seen sheep before,' said Ollie.

'Well, I've never seen sheep, but I *have* eaten lamb chops,' said Bengal. 'Delicious!' He looked towards the field of sheep.

'No way!' said Harry. 'Come on!'

They travelled quietly beside the hedge so as not to scare the sheep. All was quiet on Malone's farm.

At last they reached the mill.

Barny and Otus sat high in a chestnut tree keeping a look out while they got the flour.

Harry decided to test out the flour disguise, so he leapt off the tiger's back and straight into the white mound.

The others watched him rolling over and over. A few 'achoos' came from the flour, and with each one a small puffy white cloud rose into the air.

Then Harry reappeared. 'How do I look?'

'Different!' said Sammy.

Harry went to see himself in a small rain-pool. 'I look like a ghost! A spooky hedgehog!'

They all laughed. Then Harry
jumped into the pool and splashed
around until all the flour was
washed off.

'Your turn now, Bengal,' said
Ollie.

Bengal padded over to the
mound of flour and lay down on
his tummy. Then he rolled over
and over like a kitten, sending
large puffs of flour everywhere.

'This *is* fun!' he said, as he
wriggled around. 'How do I look?'

'You missed lots of places,' said
Harry. 'We'd better help you.'

So they all began to fling flour at
the tiger, trying to find the right
spots. Harry sat on Bengal's tail

while Sammy covered it with flour.

There was a lot of sneezing and coughing!

At last he was covered. He was completely white!

'You look just like a large pet cat,' said Harry. 'Or a large ghost,' he added.

Suddenly there was a loud shriek. It was Barny warning them that two dogs had sneaked up from the farm. The dogs were snarling and growling.

Bengal stood in fright, trembling. The others didn't know what to do – run for it or stay with the tiger.

The dogs came closer, teeth flashing. At that, Sammy jumped to the top of the mill roof.

Harry rolled himself into a ball.

Barny and Otus circled above the dogs trying to distract them.

Suddenly Sammy leapt from the roof on to Bengal's back! He grabbed hold of the tiger's tail and sank his teeth into it.

Bengal gave such a roar that the dogs turned and fled. They raced to their kennels and went into hiding!

'Well done, Bengal!' said Renny.

'It was Sammy really,' said the tiger.

'Imagine! Two dogs being afraid of a cat!' said Harry, and they all laughed.

'Let's get back to Old Lepus and see how we've done,' said Ollie.

There was Old Lepus having breakfast with Bentley. So they all joined in and had another great picnic.

'You know, it's not a good idea for all of you to go to the harbour,' said Old Lepus. 'It's too far and too dangerous.'

It was decided that Sammy Squirrel should be the one to go with Bengal. Sammy was quick, and could get out of trouble fairly easily.

'You'd better be off before the men come prowling around,' said Lepus. 'Keep to the hedgerows and when you get to the road watch out for the cars and lorries. We don't want any more accidents.'

'You'll be fine,' said Renny.

'As long as it doesn't rain!' said Harry.

'Thank you all very much,' said Bengal. There were tears in his eyes. 'I never had such good friends! I'm sort of sorry to go, but I do want to see my family.'

'Well,' said Harry, 'you were a roaring success in the circus – and you're a roaring success with us too!'

They all cheered and clapped.

Sammy climbed up on the tiger's back. Bengal padded slowly away,

looking back to see his friends
waving goodbye.

They moved out of the woods
and across the fields then up to the

road. A few cars passed. Then, when things were quiet, Bengal went onto the road and cantered along the side with Sammy keeping a look out.

They moved quickly. Then Bengal stopped suddenly. 'Look.' He pointed. Ahead was a roadside café where some people sat, eating. 'What'll we do now?'

He crept along cautiously, then Sammy had an idea.

He pointed to the lorries stopped at the café. 'We can take a ride in one of those. I bet they're going to the city.'

'You're right,' agreed Bengal. 'Let's try it.'

They found a truck with an
opening at the back. Bengal leaped
up and hid inside.

Sammy climbed on top and sat
watching for the driver.

After a while a man came out and

got into the front of the lorry. The engine started up. Soon they were on their way.

The journey took a long, long time. The animals were glad they weren't walking.

At last they reached the city. When the lorry stopped at traffic lights, they jumped out and hurried across the road.

A woman stopped and said to her husband, 'Look! That's the biggest cat I've ever seen – or is it a dog?' But it was gone before he turned to look.

Bengal and Sammy hid down a laneway. Two herring gulls were there, squabbling over a piece of bread, and Sammy called to them. 'Can you tell us where the harbour is?'

'Of course,' they said. 'Just look at our relations over there.'

They looked and saw the birds circling around. Keeping their eyes on the birds, Bengal and Sammy soon found the harbour.

'Now to find the right ship,' said Bengal.

A kittiwake flew beside them.

'Would you happen to know which boat goes to India?' asked Sammy.

The bird circled and circled above the boats then landed on the deck of one boat.

'This one,' she called.

Cautiously, they moved down the pier. The ship seemed very far out.

'Can you jump as far as that?' said
Sammy.

'Yes,' said Bengal. 'This is where
my circus training comes in handy.'

There were tears in his eyes once
more as he said goodbye to Sammy.

'Goodbye, my friend,' said
Sammy. 'Have a safe journey home.'

Bengal crouched, then sprang from the pier. He landed softly on the deck, and, with one last glance back at Sammy, he set off to find a good hiding place.

Sammy climbed onto a fence and waited until the sailors came. Then the boat sailed off into the distance.

Sammy felt a warm glow inside. Bengal was on his way home.

*   *   *

When Sammy got back to the woods, they were all waiting for news of the journey.

'Well, he's safely on a ship, anyway,' announced Sammy.

'Let's hope he gets home,' said Old Lepus.

'Things will seem very quiet around here now,' said Renny.

'You can say that again,' said
Harry, pointing to Barny and Otus
who were sound asleep on the
bough of a beech tree.

*   *   *

Early one spring morning a swallow arrived with news. Bengal had got safely home to India and he would never forget his good friends in the woods.

He had sent a gift for them. It was a shiny stone that he had found in the jungle. They gave it to Old Lepus, who said it was a jewel, and he put it in his window where they could all see it and be reminded of their good friend – the Tiger Who Was a Roaring Success!

Other books by Don Conroy in the WOODLAND FRIENDS series

THE HEDGEHOG'S PRICKLY PROBLEM
Written and illustrated by Don Conroy

Harry Hedgehog is bored with his life so he joins the circus to find adventure. But he ends up in a *very* prickly situation! Can his woodland friends rescue him?

Paperback £3.99/€5.07/$7.95

THE BAT WHO WAS ALL IN A FLAP
Written and illustrated by Don Conroy

Did you ever hear of a flying fox? Well, Harry Hedgehog actually sees one! He thinks he's going quite batty, but his woodland friends help solve the mystery ...

Paperback £3.99/€5.07/$7.95

THE OWL WHO COULDN'T GIVE A HOOT

Written and illustrated by Don Conroy

Barny Owl is very upset at not being able to HOOT, so Sammy Squirrel and his woodland friends set out to find a hoot for him! But they, and Barny, are in for a big surprise!

Paperback £3.99/€5.07/$7.95

ALSO BY DON CONROY

CARTOON FUN

Written and illustrated by Don Conroy

An easy, step-by-step guide to creating fabulous, funny and fantastic cartoons by artist, wildlife expert and TV personality Don Conroy. Begin with Don's simple shapes and in no time at all dolphins, dinosaurs, witches and monsters will be flowing from your fingertips. Soon you will be able to create your very own comic strip characters and have fun drawing caricatures of your family and friends.

The ideal book to introduce the budding artist to the wonderful world of cartooning.

Paperback £4.99/€6.34/$7.95

WILDLIFE FUN
Written and illustrated by Don Conroy

Once you've mastered *Cartoon Fun*, why not turn your hand to *Wildlife Fun*? Don Conroy shows you how to create lively and true-to-life drawings as well as cartoon animals. He provides failsafe instructions and inspiring models to follow. Includes lots of information on the lives and homes of the animals. Full of fascinating fun.

Paperback £4.99/€6.34/$7.95

Send for our full-colour catalogue

ORDER FORM

Please send me the books as marked.

I enclose cheque/postal order for £ . . . . (+£1.00 P&P per title)

OR please charge my credit card ☐ Access/Mastercard ☐ Visa

Card Number _ _ _ _ ' _ _ _ _ _ _ _ _ _ _ _ _

Expiry Date _ _ / _ _

Name. . . . . Tel . . . .

Address . . . .

. . . .

Please send orders to: THE O'BRIEN PRESS, 20 Victoria Road, Dublin 6.

Tel: +353 1 4923333; Fax: + 353 1 4922777; E-mail: books@obrien.ie

Website: www.obrien.ie

Note: prices subject to change without notice